A Puppy is for Loving

Mary Labatt

illustrated by Renata Liwska

ORCA BOOK PUBLISHERS

To my grandmother, Sarah Morgan.

Text copyright © 2007 Mary Labatt
Illustrations copyright © 2007 Renata Liwska

Library and Archives Canada Cataloguing in Publication

Labatt, Mary, 1944-
A puppy is for loving / written by Mary Labatt; illustrated by Renata Liwska.

(Orca echoes)
ISBN 978-1-55143-477-3

1. Puppies--Juvenile fiction. I. Liwska, Renata II. Title. III. Series.

PS8573.A135P86 2007   jC813'.54   C2007-903962-6

First published in the United States, 2007
Library of Congress Control Number: 2007930929

Summary: Elizabeth watches her grandma's collie birth six puppies, and then she helps to find homes for each and every one.

Orca Book Publishers gratefully acknowledges the support for its publishing programs provided by the following agencies: the Government of Canada through the Book Publishing Industry Development Program and the Canada Council for the Arts, and the Province of British Columbia through the BC Arts Council and the Book Publishing Tax Credit.

Typesetting by Teresa Bubela
Cover artwork and interior illustrations by Renata Liwska

ORCA BOOK PUBLISHERS
PO Box 5626, STN. B
VICTORIA, BC CANADA
V8R 6S4

ORCA BOOK PUBLISHERS
PO Box 468
CUSTER, WA USA
98240-0468

www.orcabook.com
Printed and bound in Canada.
Printed on 100% PCW recycled paper.

010 09 08 07 • 4 3 2 1

Contents

Chapter 1: Elsie's Surprise 1

Chapter 2: The Whelping Box 6

Chapter 3: A Den for Elsie 11

Chapter 4: Waiting for Puppies 16

Chapter 5: Elsie's Miracle 20

Chapter 6: Looking After Puppies 26

Chapter 7: Getting to Know Each Puppy ... 31

Chapter 8: A Family for Gloria 36

Chapter 9: Clementine and Emily 42

Chapter 10: Someone for Princess 46

Chapter 11: What about Grandma? 49

Chapter 12: Annabel is not Lucky 52

Chapter 13: The Luckiest Puppy of All 56

Chapter 1
Elsie's Surprise

It was summer. And every summer I went to my grandmother's farm. I couldn't wait to get there. As we drove up the long drive to the farmhouse I saw Grandma standing under the maple trees with her dog, Elsie.

My grandmother hugged us. Elsie barked.

Then Grandma led us into her big farm kitchen. I could smell fresh bread. The shiny wood floors squeaked. A breeze ruffled the curtains. Outside birds sang in the cornfields.

I climbed the wooden stairs to my blue and white bedroom. Upstairs the house smelled of lavender. When I threw down my backpack the bed creaked.

1

I put my clothes in the old dresser. Flowered paper lined the drawers.

I could hear my parents and my grandma talking in the kitchen.

"You should live closer to us, Mom," said my dad.

"Yes," said my mother, "you must be lonely here."

I held my breath.

Would my grandmother leave this magic place? Would she leave this place where my father and my uncles grew up? Would she leave this place where my Grandpa Fred died?

"I can't leave," said Grandma. Her voice was clear and strong. "I feel close to your father here. If you pull me up, I'll be like a tree with no roots."

My mother and father talked on and on about apartments in the city. They said she would like it there.

But Grandma just said no. "My roots are here," she told them.

After lunch it was time for my parents to leave. Grandma and Elsie and I stood on the porch and waved. We watched the car wind down the lane.

I held Grandma's hand. Together we watched the car go over the hill. The sun felt warm on my head. We were alone now. Elsie sat quietly with us in the silence of the farm.

"Well, Elizabeth," said Grandma at last. "You're here. And what a wonderful summer this will be."

I looked up at my grandmother's kind face. Her bright blue eyes twinkled. "I have a surprise this summer," she said.

I held my breath. I loved surprises. Elsie thumped her tail.

"You will never guess this surprise," said Grandma.

"What is it?" I couldn't wait to find out.

But Grandma just smiled.

"Tell me, Grandma."

"Well...," said Grandma. The corners of her mouth twitched.

"What is it?" I cried.

"It's about Elsie," said Grandma, "and it's a very nice surprise."

I waited. Grandma smiled down at Elsie, and then she looked back at me.

"Elsie is expecting puppies in three days!"

Chapter 2
The Whelping Box

I looked at Elsie.

Elsie looked the same. She had the same beautiful long nose and the same warm brown eyes. She had the same golden fur and the same white mane.

Grandma put her hand on Elsie's head. "We have to get ready for the puppies," she said. "Elsie needs us."

Elsie poked her nose into my hand.

That afternoon Elsie and I went to all my favorite places on the farm. We went to the creek. We waded in the cool mud. I swung on the old rope that my dad used to swing on.

I listened for a moment. I thought I could hear the shouts of my father and his brothers from long ago.

That must be what Grandma hears, I thought. That must be what she means by "roots."

After supper my grandmother asked me to help her. We dragged two big cartons from the shed.

"This is a whelping box," said Grandma. "We need to put it together."

"What's a whelping box?" I asked.

"It's the box where Elsie will give birth to her puppies," explained Grandma.

I didn't see why Elsie would go in a big box.

Grandma and I dragged the cartons to the dining room. "Elsie wants a secret place to have puppies," Grandma said. She pushed the chairs and table back to the wall.

"What's wrong with the kitchen?" I asked.

My grandma shook her head. "Not secret enough. Elsie will worry if someone comes to the door. She needs a room of her own."

Elsie watched while we pulled out pieces of a big box. She watched while we clipped them together.

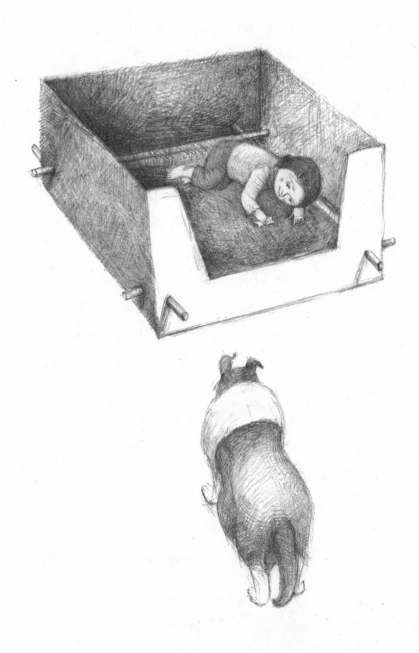

The whelping box looked like a big square with a rug in it. It was about eight feet long and eight feet wide. Grandma got some old sheets and put them in the box on the rug.

"Now," she said, "you go in the whelping box with dog cookies. You can show Elsie that this is a good place."

I hopped in the whelping box and sat down. I showed Elsie the dog cookies. She stepped in the box with me.

"Elsie needs to get used to the whelping box," said Grandma. "Maybe you should lie down so that she can see you like it."

Grandma sat in her rocking chair to watch.

Elsie and I played for a long time. In and out of the whelping box we went. I took Elsie's chewy bone in there. I gave her lots of cookies.

Suddenly Elsie stood up. She clawed at the sheets. She whipped them into a pile.

"What's wrong with Elsie?" I cried.

Elsie scratched and scratched.

"She's nesting," said Grandma. She sat back in her rocking chair.

Elsie was trying to pull up the rug in the whelping box.

"What's nesting?" I asked.

Elsie turned round and round. She scratched and scratched.

Grandma smiled. "Elsie knows puppies are coming. She's making a nest for them." Grandma rocked back and forth.

We watched Elsie scratch for a long time. At last she lay down on the pile of sheets.

That night I went up to bed in my little room. But Elsie stayed downstairs in the whelping box. A breeze blew the curtains. I lay still and listened to the crickets. Downstairs Elsie was scratching.

My heart soared at the thought of puppies.

Chapter 3
A Den for Elsie

When I woke up, the sun was shining bright and warm. Flies buzzed in the window. Far-off tractors rumbled in the fields. Dishes clinked in the kitchen.

I went down to the kitchen. "Good morning, sleepy," said my grandmother. She held out a plate. "Have a muffin. I just made them."

I peeked into the dining room. Elsie was snoozing on her nest in the whelping box. She opened her eyes and wagged her tail. She stood up to be petted.

"She seems to like the whelping box," said Grandma. "So far we've done a good job."

Elsie licked my hand.

All day we got ready for Elsie's puppies. My grandmother put another rocking chair beside the whelping box. "We can wait together," she said.

She got a pile of clean towels. "We need towels to dry the new puppies," she said.

She put a heating pad in the bottom of a basket. Then she folded a towel over the heating pad. "This will keep the newborn puppies warm," she said.

Then she got scissors. "If Elsie doesn't chew off the puppy's sac, we'll cut it open," she said.

"Ugh," I said.

"If Elsie doesn't chew the cord, we'll cut it."

"Yuck," I said.

Grandma just smiled. She put out dental floss. "We'll tie the cord with dental floss," she went on.

"Aagh," I said. My stomach rolled.

Grandma set out a bag of cotton puffs and a bottle of iodine. "We'll put iodine on the cord to kill germs."

I shivered. I didn't want to cut puppies out of sacs. I didn't want to cut cords. I wondered if people ever fainted when they were doing this.

But Elsie looked up at me with soft brown eyes. She needed me. So I didn't say anything.

"Now," said my grandmother. "Elsie needs a den like a wild dog."

"Where does a wild dog get a den?" I asked.

"They dig a hole or go in a cave," said Grandma.

"Do we have to dig a hole?" I asked.

"No," said Grandma, "we're going to put a roof on the whelping box. That will make a cave."

Grandma got a sheet. Then she got some big books. She asked me to hold the sheet on the table. She put a big book on each corner. Then she pulled the other side of the sheet to the buffet. She put books on that side too. We pulled the sheet tight so it didn't sag into Elsie's box. It made a good roof.

My grandmother grinned. "Now Elsie has her own den."

Elsie wagged her tail and hopped into the whelping box. She scratched her sheets. Then she lay down on them. She looked out at us from under her roof.

My grandmother smiled. "Now we wait for the puppies."

Chapter 4
Waiting for Puppies

All day we stayed home. We sat on the porch. We worked in the garden. We sat in the rocking chairs beside the whelping box. Elsie kept making new nests.

My grandmother picked up her knitting. "Puppies often come at night," she said.

She rocked back and forth. "I think it's because it's so quiet at night."

I pulled the dining room curtains. I turned off the TV in the kitchen. I wanted Elsie to think it was night. Only the clicking of knitting needles broke the stillness.

I was worried. "What if the puppies don't come tonight?"

Grandma was calm. "We'll just wait. I think Elsie is ready."

Elsie was lying on her nest.

"How do you know?" I asked. Elsie didn't look very ready.

"She wouldn't eat her food today," said Grandma. "That's a sign that the puppies are ready to be born."

Grandma looked at Elsie. "When Elsie starts to pant, we'll see a big gush of water. Then the puppies will start coming." She smiled at me. "We might have to stay up all night."

I sat back in my rocker to wait. I had a book to read, but I didn't care about the story. All I could think about was puppies.

The clock ticked. Grandma click-clacked her knitting needles. Elsie got up again and again. Over and over she pawed her sheets up into a new shape. Then she lay down. Every time Elsie did that, Grandma winked at me.

17

The room grew darker. Night sounds came through the open windows.

My grandmother got up to close the windows. "New puppies can't have a draft," she said.

All at once it happened. I heard a gush of water.

Elsie whirled around to look at her tail. Water spread over the sheets.

Grandma put her fingers to her lips. "We must be very quiet and very calm," she whispered. She stood up. "First, I need to take the wet sheets away."

"Why?" I asked.

"A new puppy could get tangled in the sheets. Then it would smother." Grandma pulled the sheets gently away from Elsie.

Elsie paced back and forth in the whelping box.

She lay down and looked at her tail. She nosed under her tail.

We waited.

Chapter 5
Elsie's Miracle

"The first puppy is coming," whispered my grandmother. "Hand me a towel."

I handed her a towel.

A black lump appeared behind Elsie.

"That's the sac," whispered Grandma. "If Elsie doesn't open it, we will."

Elsie whipped around. She bit the black lump open. Out came a tiny wet puppy.

The puppy was wet brown. Its eyes were scrunched shut. It had a little mask over its eyes like a raccoon.

"Elsie will chew the cord now," whispered Grandma.

And Elsie did. We waited while Elsie licked her puppy all over.

"The first few minutes belong to Elsie," my grandmother said. "She is getting to know her new puppy."

Then Grandma picked up the tiny puppy very gently. She dried it with a fluffy towel. She dabbed some iodine on the cord stump.

Grandma put the tiny puppy on Elsie's nipple. She squeezed Elsie's nipple. I saw a little drop of white milk.

Grandma rubbed the puppy's mouth on the milk. A tiny, tiny pink tongue came out.

"This first milk is important," said Grandma. "It will make the puppy strong."

The new puppy began to suck.

Elsie nosed the puppy and licked and licked. It fell off the nipple. Grandma put the puppy on another nipple. After a while the puppy snuggled into Elsie's belly and slept.

Grandma picked the puppy up. She put it in the basket on the heating pad. "We don't want Elsie to roll on the puppy," she whispered.

"When will the next one come?" I asked.

"We just have to wait," said Grandma. "Sometimes it takes two hours."

So I sat back to wait. It was a long, long night. In the quiet of the dining room, I dozed.

The next puppy was black with brown spots over its eyes.

I dozed again. Three times I woke to see Grandma

drying a new puppy. But I could never stay awake to see the next one come.

Elsie had six puppies that night. One puppy was a sable like her. The other five puppies were black with white chests and feet. They had little brown spots over their closed eyes.

"Why are they black?" I asked.

"They look like their father," said Grandma. "He's a beautiful tri-colored collie with a white chest. He has a huge white mane."

One of the black puppies was tiny and skinny. When Grandma put it on Elsie's nipple, it didn't want to suck.

"This is the runt," said Grandma. "We'll take extra care of her."

When all the puppies had come, Elsie stopped panting. Six puppies slept in the basket on the heating pad.

"We can take Elsie outside now," said Grandma. "We'll give her some good food."

We called Elsie out of the whelping box. Elsie didn't want to leave her new puppies, but at last she came.

We stepped out into the silence of a new day. Dawn streaked across the sky in a blaze of pink, red and orange. I felt as if we were in a church.

We had just seen the miracle of birth. Neither of us could speak.

Elsie walked through the beauty of the dawn. She moved gracefully—like someone who had a wonderful secret.

Grandma gave Elsie a gravy-soaked dinner. After her food, Elsie drank a long, long drink of water. Then she went back to the door and scratched.

She whined to go back to her puppies.

Chapter 6
Looking After Puppies

When she got back to the whelping box, Elsie poked each puppy with her nose.

"She's counting them!" I whispered.

Grandma smiled. "Elsie will do that every time she comes back."

Elsie lay down on her side. We put each puppy on a nipple. They all started to suck. The puppies were so tiny they looked like little guinea pigs.

"How do they know how to suck?" I asked.

"It's a miracle. We see miracles every day, but we don't notice."

Grandma pointed to the runt. "Look! The little one is sucking!"

I felt sorry for the tiny runt, squirming and sucking at Elsie's nipple. "She looks too small, Grandma."

"We'll make sure she gets extra food," said my grandmother.

"Will she die?"

"I hope not," said Grandma. "We'll do everything we can. We'll let her feed by herself. And we'll give her a bottle sometimes."

"Now, Elsie needs to be alone with her puppies," my grandmother told me.

We tiptoed out of the dining room. And we closed the door for Elsie. We stepped out into the quiet morning. We sat on the porch chairs, thinking of the puppies.

After that the days went by slowly.

Elsie ate extra food three times a day. Grandma and I cooked hamburger for her. Elsie loved it.

Elsie walked around the house with me. But she wouldn't stay outside for long. She always wanted to go back to her puppies. We didn't explore the farm anymore. Every time I tried to go for a walk, Elsie stopped and trotted back to the house. She scratched at the door to see her puppies.

We kept the dining room dark like a real den. Elsie felt safe.

I sat in the rocker for long hours. And I watched Elsie care for her babies. She washed them with her tongue. She lay on her side and fed them. She nudged them over on their backs to clean them.

Sometimes a puppy crawled behind Elsie's back. Then I picked it up. I put it in front of Elsie so she wouldn't roll on it.

Three times a day, I put five of the puppies in the basket. Then I let the little runt feed by herself. Once a day I held her in my arms and fed her a bottle. It was special milk from the vet. The little runt got stronger every day.

At night we got up to check the puppies. We had to see if one had rolled behind Elsie. We had to make sure they were all warm.

Before we went to bed we turned on a heat lamp. Every morning we found all six puppies right under the lamp. They slept in a little pile.

"What will we do with six puppies?" I asked my grandmother one day.

"We'll find people who need them."

"Need them?" I was surprised. "What can puppies do for people?"

Grandma smiled her slow smile. Her kind eyes were soft.

"A puppy is for loving, Elizabeth. We will find people who need a puppy to love," she said.

I thought about what my grandmother said. The puppies were crawling now with their eyes scrunched shut.

Were there six people in the world who needed a puppy to love?

Chapter 7
Getting to Know
Each Puppy

I loved those quiet hours with the puppies. I sat and watched them. I got to know each puppy. And I gave them names.

The tri-colored male was a tough guy. He always pushed his sisters away from the nipple. I called him Rocky.

One little tri female was soft and gentle. She always crawled to my voice. She wouldn't feed until I cuddled her. I called her Emily.

Another little tri female squeaked and squeaked. Sometimes she sounded like a chicken squawking. I decided to name her Annabel.

The biggest one was the sable. I called her Clementine. I got the name from a song about Clementine with big feet.

I called the little tri-colored runt Princess, because she got so much attention. Even with her eyes scrunched shut she looked as if she expected servants.

I called the most beautiful one Gloria. She was black with a huge white mane. I picked that name because Grandma said her mane would be glorious.

The days went by and the puppies grew. I talked to each one and called each one by name. One by one they opened their eyes.

They crawled all over the whelping box. But they always ended up in a heap. When they were four weeks old, the puppies were ready to eat food. Elsie was going to get some time off.

My grandmother showed me how to make puppy mush. We chopped up puppy kibble in the blender. We mixed it with beef baby food and powdered animal milk from the pet store. Then we stirred in warm water to make mush.

Princess wouldn't eat. She turned up her royal nose. She looked at me as if I were giving her garbage.

Rocky pushed everybody out of the way. He stuck his nose in the bowl and slurped.

Emily came to me and waited. I picked her up and fussed over her. As soon as I put her down she ate.

Gloria nibbled. Her manners were as beautiful as she was.

Annabel was a pig.

Clementine pushed in beside Rocky and gobbled right along with him.

When the puppies were full, they drank water. Then they flopped down in a heap.

Still, Princess hadn't eaten. When I put her near the bowl, she turned up her tiny nose. I got a spoon and put some mush on it. I held her in my arms and talked softly to her. Then I put the spoon up to her nose. At last she stuck out her tiny pink tongue.

Soon they were big enough to move out to the shed, whelping box and all.

While I walked around the farm with Elsie, my grandmother talked on the telephone. She put ads in all the newspapers for the puppies. Grandma said she wasn't going to let any puppy go to a home where it was not needed. Grandma and I agreed.

We were going to be very fussy with Elsie's children.

Chapter 8
A Family for Gloria

We wanted the perfect family for each puppy.

"Princess will need a palace," I joked.

Grandma smiled. "We'll know when Princess's family turns up," she said.

The phone started to ring. I could hear my grandmother on the phone, talking to people.

"No, one of our puppies would not suit you," she said one day. She put the phone down.

"What's wrong, Grandma?" I asked.

"Hmph," she said. "That woman is not even sure she likes collies. She just wants to try one out!"

"That doesn't sound right." I was puzzled.

"Of course it's not right," said my grandmother.

"A puppy needs people who want him. Not someone who wants to try him out!"

I understood. We needed people who wanted to love a puppy.

"Let's be tough on people, Grandma," I said. "I don't want any of Elsie's babies to be unhappy."

Grandma folded her arms. "We'll wait for the right people if we have to wait all year." She looked firm. "You have my word on that."

So we waited.

One day the phone rang.

An old man who lived alone was calling. He'd had collies all his life, he said. When he was a boy in Wales he'd had his first collie. And a beauty she was too. Now his old collie had died. He needed another one badly.

"They're part of my life. I'm lonely without one," he explained.

"He should have Gloria," I told my grandmother that night.

"Why Gloria?" she asked.

"Because she's so beautiful. He would take her for walks and brush her. He would show her off to all the people in his town."

"Maybe..." My grandmother wasn't sure. "He's coming tomorrow. We'll see which puppy is right for him."

The next day a dusty car rattled up the lane. When it stopped an old man got out. He reached back into the car for his cane. He limped over to us.

We took him to the shed to see the puppies. There was a rush of feet as all the puppies ran to see who was there. They all put their paws on the edge of the whelping box and looked out.

And then it happened. Gloria jumped and whined and yelped at the old man.

His eyes filled with tears. "Why, she's the spitting image of my Betsy when I was a lad!"

Gloria yelped and yelped.

"May I pick her up?" the old man asked. Tears slipped down his cheeks.

My grandmother nodded.

The old man picked up Gloria and nuzzled her
with his nose. She nuzzled back.

I saw the magic. It was as if Grandma and I were
not in the shed anymore. It was just this old man and

Gloria—nuzzling and nuzzling. He spoke softly in her tiny ear.

My grandmother winked at me. She told me to come outside. "Let's leave them alone for a few minutes," she said.

Outside Grandma whispered, "I think you were right, Elizabeth. I think he belongs with Gloria."

And so Gloria found her family.

When the old man carried Gloria to his car, she never looked back. She snuggled down in the basket beside him. She gazed up at him with adoring eyes.

"They belong together," said Grandma.

My grandmother was happy. "He has a heart full of love to give Gloria. And he needs her. His wife is dead, and he lives alone. Gloria will help him live with his loss."

Grandma looked at me with those wise blue eyes of hers. She cocked her head to one side. "How did you know Gloria was the one for him?"

"I don't know," I said. "It was just a feeling."

I looked out to the road where the car had gone over the hill. I felt sad losing Gloria. She was the beauty of the family. But I knew she was home.

Inside the phone was ringing. Grandma rushed to answer it.

"Let's hope that's a family for one of the others," she said.

Chapter 9
Clementine and Emily

And so it went. Each day someone new came to see the puppies.

If my grandmother didn't like the way the people talked, she told them the puppies were all sold. Then the people left. And Grandma told me why they couldn't have one of our puppies.

I understood. The puppies were counting on us. Elsie was counting on us.

Clementine was the next one to find her family. She was the big sable pup. Big fat Clemmie was born to have fun. She hid on her brother and sisters. She jumped out at them. She zigzagged around the yard until they chased her. Clemmie didn't wag her tail.

She wiggled her whole behind. She had a big white splotch on her nose.

A twelve-year-old girl came with her parents. She fell in love with Clemmie. Clemmie jumped up in the girl's lap. She licked and licked and licked. The girl giggled. Clemmie wiggled.

It felt right. The family had a cat and an older dog at home. Clemmie would have friends to play with every day.

In the car, Clemmie looked back as if she were saying a happy good-bye.

"That's two families!" said my grandmother. "We need four more."

I looked in the whelping box. Rocky, Annabel, Emily and Princess looked back at me. Where would they go? Would they be happy?

That night my grandmother was on the phone for a long time. Her voice was soft. I heard her say, "A puppy will help you to heal."

She put down the phone, and she told me the woman's collie had just died. The woman was so sad she was afraid to love another dog. But she missed her collie so much.

"A puppy will help you," my grandmother had told her.

But the woman wasn't sure.

The next day the woman called back. She asked if we had a puppy with a lot of love to give.

"I'll find just the puppy for you," my grandmother said. Grandma looked at me. "Which puppy has the most love to give?" she asked.

"Emily!" I cried. "Emily won't even eat until I hug her!"

Emily was special. When I held her I could feel her love. It was the best feeling in the world.

And so Emily's new family came. The broken-hearted woman got out of the car. She looked scared. Her husband followed her. When she saw Emily, her eyes filled with tears. She picked Emily up. Tears splashed on Emily's glossy fur.

Emily lifted her tiny head and licked the tears. The more the woman cried, the more Emily snuggled.

My grandmother and I were crying too. "You will be happy with Emily," my grandmother said.

Grandma wiped tears from her cheeks. "Emily will help you. You will never forget your dog. But it won't hurt so much now."

And so Emily went away from us to a home filled with love.

Chapter 10
Someone for Princess

Princess and Rocky and Annabel were sad that night. They didn't play or romp or jump. They looked at us with sad eyes.

"They miss their sisters," I said.

The next day the puppies perked up. They chased each other around the lawn. Princess was still eating from a spoon. She still turned up her nose at the puppy bowl.

"I hope a queen comes for her," I said.

"She doesn't need a queen," said my grandmother firmly. "She needs someone who needs her."

And so they came. Two children who had just lost their grandfather drove up with their parents.

They looked at the puppies with sad eyes.

Princess sat up and looked at the children with her sharp brown eyes.

Turning in circles and running with little hops, Princess jumped so much she jumped right out of the whelping box.

"I can't believe she did that!" cried Grandma. The children giggled.

Princess zigzagged all over the yard. She picked up a toy and tossed it in the air. She nipped at their ankles. She growled like a lion. The children laughed and laughed. Rocky and Annabel watched with a puzzled look.

"She's the perfect puppy!" shouted the children. They ran. Princess chased them. Princess tripped and did a somersault.

"We want her!" shouted the children.

Princess barked and barked.

At last the family climbed into the car. Princess snuggled between the children. She sighed.

Princess was home.

Chapter 11
What about Grandma?

For the next three days Rocky and Annabel played together. They growled. They wrestled. They took turns being the boss. Then they flopped on the grass.

That night in my blue and white bedroom, I thought about the puppies. All the people had called to say how wonderful their puppies were. But I didn't feel happy. Something was bothering me.

This summer had been full of life and full of joy. Now I had to go back to school. Rocky and Annabel had to go to new homes.

It wasn't right for all six beautiful puppies to go out into the world to love other people. Elsie would

lose all her children. And there would be no puppy left for my grandmother.

The long winter was coming. Grandma and Elsie would be all alone. I knew Grandma was lonely. She couldn't fool me. I saw her sitting in Grandpa's workshop picking up his tools. My grandmother had a broken heart, but she would not speak of it.

She always sat on the porch and looked out at the farm. I knew she could see my dad playing in the yard. I knew she could see Grandpa working in the fields. That was what she meant by roots. No wonder my grandmother wouldn't leave.

But I wished she and Elsie had someone to stay with them.

Chapter 12
Annabel is not Lucky

That's when Annabel and I began to have an understanding.

I whispered in her tiny floppy ear. I looked into her bright black eyes. Annabel seemed to know. Someone should stay with my grandmother. Someone should stay with Elsie. It couldn't be me. I had to go back to school.

Annabel's bright eyes flickered. It had to be her.

From then on, I held my breath every time the phone rang.

Most times my grandmother said, "No, one of our puppies would not be right you." Then one day

I heard her say, "Come and see Rocky. I think he's perfect for you."

A young couple came up the winding drive. Their collie had been killed in the forest by wolves. They were sick with sorrow that they let their dog run free.

They came with toys for Rocky. He seemed to know that this was his family. He ran and jumped and flipped over in excitement.

"Rocky is just the start of our family," said the young couple.

"Next year we'll get another puppy. Then we'll have children. Dogs and kids—that's what we want."

Rocky looked as if he had gone to dog heaven. He seemed to grin out the car window as they drove away.

Then there was Annabel—only Annabel who had not found a family.

"Annabel is not lucky," said my grandmother. "Nobody came for her."

I watched Elsie licking Annabel. They turned over and over with love.

"Maybe she's the luckiest puppy of all," I said.

Grandma was puzzled. "What do you mean?"

"Maybe she should stay with you, Grandma," I said.

Grandma listened.

"You need her," I said. "Elsie needs her."

Still Grandma listened.

"Maybe the farm won't be so lonely this winter if Annabel stays."

My grandmother opened her mouth to tell me that she was not lonely. But she closed her mouth. She didn't speak. She watched Annabel roll over and over with her mother.

"We'll see who comes," Grandma said quietly.

Chapter 13
The Luckiest Puppy of All

But no one came.

At last my parents came to get me. It was time for me to go home. It was time for school.

When I went up to pack I heard them talking downstairs. It was the same talk.

"But, Mom," said my father, "it's lonely here in the winter. You can't stay here."

"You would love it in the city," said my mother.

Grandma was firm. "My memories are here. I will never leave."

My father sounded sad. "Memories aren't enough, Mom."

"That's right," said my mother. "You need your family near you."

"Everybody needs to be loved," said my father.

I didn't hear my grandmother's answer. But I knew she wouldn't leave.

When it was time to go, Grandma hugged me tight. She told me I was the best girl in all the world. She asked me to write to her this winter. I promised I would.

Then I said, "Now *you* have to promise me something, Grandma."

Grandma nodded. Her white hair was soft in the sunlight. Her lined face was kind.

"Promise me," I said, "that you will keep Annabel."

My grandmother looked at me with wise blue eyes. I held my breath.

Then she nodded. "You have my word on it, Elizabeth," said my grandmother. "I will keep Annabel."

My heart soared. Annabel was home.

We all said good-bye with hugs and kisses. My mother and my grandmother cried. I picked up Annabel and whispered in her tiny ear.

When we drove down the drive I looked back. My grandmother was waving from the porch. Elsie sat beside her like she always did. But this time there was something different.

This time Annabel played at their feet—beautiful black Annabel with her white ruff and her white paws.

I knew my grandmother would be all right this winter. My parents were worried that memories were not enough.

But my parents didn't understand. Grandma needed someone to love. Grandma had Annabel.

And a puppy is for loving.

Mary Labatt breeds collies with her daughter, Elizabeth. She has written two series of books about dogs: *Dog Detective Sam* and *Puppy Sam*. Mary lives and writes in Port Rowan, Ontario.